W9-CPF-682

Berry Fairy Tales

# Snow White

By Megan E. Bryant

Illustrated by Tonja and John Huxtable

Grosset & Dunlap

Strawberry Shortcake™ © 2007 by Those Characters From Cleveland, Inc. Used under license by Penguin Young Readers Group.
All rights reserved. Published by Grosset & Dunlap, a division of Penguin Young Readers Group, 345 Hudson Street, New York, New York 10014.
GROSSET & DUNLAP is a trademark of Penguin Group (USA) Inc. Manufactured in China.

Library of Congress Control Number: 2006016225

ISBN 978-0-448-44458-1          10 9 8 7 6 5 4 3 2 1

Once upon a time, Strawberry Shortcake and her friends planned a special day of pampering for their pets! Strawberry brushed her pets, Pupcake and Custard, until their coats gleamed, while Angel wove a wreath of flowers for Vanilla Icing to wear.

Ginger Snap dressed her pet, Chocolate Chipmunk, in a tiny hat and bowtie. "You're the berry best pet ever!" she exclaimed as she held a mirror in front of him.

The girls grew quiet. Even the pets looked sad.

"What's wrong?" Ginger Snap asked as she glanced around. "What did I do?"

"Ginger," Orange Blossom said quietly, "it's not berry nice to brag."

"You know, that reminds me of a story I heard once," Strawberry spoke up. "Once upon a time . . ."

A lovely young princess named Snow White was born in the Berry Kingdom. She had hair the color of a fiery sunrise, lips as red as berries, and skin as white as the new-fallen snow—which is how she got her name. Snow White had neither mother nor father, so Queen Gingeretta from the Spice Kingdom cared for her until the day Snow White would be old enough to rule Berry Kingdom on her own.

As the years passed, it was difficult for Queen Gingeretta to control the jealousy that swelled in her heart—especially when she thought of giving up the rule of Berry Kingdom. *Why should Snow White take Berry Kingdom from me?* she thought angrily. Queen Gingeretta demanded an answer from the magic mirror in her chambers: "Mirror, mirror, on the wall. Who is the best to rule them all?"

A rainbow mist swirled over the surface of the mirror, then revealed an image of Snow White. A hollow voice replied to the queen, "Kind and happy and fair of face, Snow White has the wisdom to rule with grace."

"Impossible!" hissed Queen Gingeretta. "I'm the best one to rule Berry Kingdom. What does Snow White know about ruling a nation? Nothing!"

Queen Gingeretta gazed out the window, wondering how she could possibly keep Berry Kingdom for herself. She spotted the castle flower girl, Orangine, picking fresh flowers for the royal chambers. Suddenly a terrible plan began to form in Queen Gingeretta's mind. She called to Orangine and ordered her to come inside.

"I have a very important task for you," Queen Gingeretta told Orangine. "Take Snow White deep into the woods to look for flowers. But you must not bring her back to Berry Kingdom. I want you to take her over the border to Wildland and leave her in the deepest, darkest part of the woods!"

"Oh, no!" began Orangine. "I could never—"

"Not another word," Queen Gingeretta interrupted sharply as she pointed to the door.

Orangine found Snow White picking berries in the castle garden.
"W-would you like to pick wildflowers in the woods with me?"
Orangine stammered.

"Of course!" the princess replied. "That sounds berry nice!"

Snow White followed Orangine deep into the woods, chattering and
laughing as the girls gathered sweetly scented flowers. But with every
step Orangine took, a terrible feeling of dread grew in her heart. At
last, she could bear it no more.

"Snow White, you must never return to Berry Kingdom!" exclaimed Orangine.

"Why? What's the matter?" Snow White asked.

"Queen Gingeretta told me to leave you in the woods of Wildland!" Orangine said urgently. "But I could never do that. Never!"

"Oh, no!" Snow White cried. "What am I going to do?"

"I know a safe place where you can hide," Orangine replied. "A tiny cottage at the edge of Berry Kingdom. No one lives there—I don't think anyone even knows about it except for me. Let's hurry—the queen must not know that I've disobeyed her!"

Snow White and Orangine ran to the border between Berry Kingdom and Wildland. "There it is!" whispered Orangine, pointing to a small cottage. "You'll be safe there." She gave Snow White a hug before hurrying home.

Snow White had never felt so scared in all her life. She cautiously walked up to the lonely little cottage. "Hello? Hello?" she called. But there was no answer. A tear slipped down her cheek as she realized how alone she was. As a pelting rain began to fall, Snow White dashed into the cottage to escape the storm.

"Who are you? And what are you doing here?" asked a voice from the shadows.

Snow White tried not to cry. "Queen Gingeretta has sent me away," she replied. "I have no home and no place to go."

Snow White heard rustling and murmuring. As her eyes adjusted to the dim light, she saw seven pairs of eyes blinking at her. Finally, a pink cat stepped forward.

"We've decided you can stay here," the cat declared. "We're the seven little friends—but we have no one to look after us."

Snow White beamed. "Oh, thank you so much!" she cried. "I would love to look after you!"

Snow White and the seven little friends soon learned to take care of one another. Snow White kept house—sweeping, mopping, dusting, and tidying—while her new friends foraged in the forest for delicious berries, nuts, and greens that were good to eat. Before long, they were living a berry happy life together.

Back at the castle, Queen Gingeretta was certain that she would rule Berry Kingdom now that Snow White was hopelessly lost in Wildland. She decided to consult the magic mirror again. "Mirror, mirror, on the wall. Who is the best to rule them all?" she asked.

The same rainbow mist swirled over the mirror. And then the mirror replied:

"Snow White is safe, in a happy place. When she returns, she'll rule with grace."

"How can this be?" Queen Gingeretta snarled as an image of Snow White appeared in the mirror. "I won't allow it!"

As the queen glared at the mirror, she was reminded of Snow White's fondness for strawberries. She began to think of another terrible plan. Queen Gingeretta raced to the deepest dungeons, where she mixed a colorless, tasteless potion. She dipped the biggest, reddest strawberry into the brew. "One bite and Snow White will fall into eternal sleep!" she laughed.

For good measure, the queen disguised herself as an old peddler woman with silver hair and a dark cloak. "She'll never recognize me now!" Queen Gingeretta proclaimed.

Queen Gingeretta hurried through the woods to the hidden cottage.
She found Snow White alone, humming happily as she tidied the cottage.
  She rapped on the door. "Bright, sweet strawberries!" the queen called.
  "My favorite!" exclaimed Snow White as she brought the strawberry to
her lips. "I love strawb—"
  Suddenly, Snow White fell to the floor. It was just as the queen had
hoped—one taste, and Snow White was lost in a deep, dreamless sleep!

By the time the seven little friends returned to the cottage with food for supper, the queen was safely back at the castle.

"What are you doing on the floor, silly?" the cat asked. But Snow White did not answer. "Snow White? Snow White!"

The little friends did everything they could to wake Snow White. They nudged her and kissed her, patted her face, and banged on pots and pans to make noise. But she did not stir.

With heavy hearts, the little friends realized that Snow White was under an enchantment. There was nothing they could do to help her. Sadly, they made a bed of flowers and trailing vines in a clearing near the cottage. They laid Snow White upon this bower, where the sun would shine upon her and the cool breezes would whisper in her ears. For many long days and nights the friends attended the sleeping Snow White in hopes that she would wake—but she never did.

Back at the castle, Queen Gingeretta began to plan a royal party to celebrate becoming queen of Berry Kingdom. She misled people throughout the land by saying that Snow White had run away rather than take her place as ruler. It seemed certain that Berry Kingdom would soon fall to Queen Gingeretta's wicked plan.

But the mirror still knew the truth. Whenever Queen Gingeretta passed by its shiny surface, an image of the sleeping Snow White bloomed across it. The guilt deep in Queen Gingeretta's heart was soon entangled with fear. What would become of her if the people of Berry Kingdom ever learned what she had done?

The fearful queen had no choice. "You! And you! Cover all the mirrors!" she shouted at the servants. "I want no reflections in this castle!"

Soon the mirrors were shrouded with thick, velvet drapes. No reflections could be seen—and Snow White's fate was hidden from all who lived in the castle.

It was soon time for the royal coronation. All the people of the Berry Kingdom and neighboring lands were in attendance, including brave Prince Huckleberry. They gathered in the ballroom awaiting Queen Gingeretta's arrival.

The queen, dressed in her finest gown, prepared for her royal entrance. Majestically she swept into the ballroom, ready to greet her new subjects.

Instead, she found Snow White's image surrounding her on every mirror in the ballroom!

"Who removed the drapes? Who?" shrieked the queen.

"I did!" cried Orangine. "I thought—for the coronation—"

"Never mind that!" interrupted Prince Huckleberry. "What has happened to Snow White? Where is she?"

Queen Gingeretta could keep her terrible secret no longer. "She's in an enchanted sleep at the edge of the woods!" she sobbed. "I've done a terrible thing. I wanted to rule Berry Kingdom all by myself!"

"What's important now is that we save Snow White," Prince Huckleberry said firmly.

"I know the way to the cottage!" Orangine spoke up.

"Then you must take us there at once!" declared Prince Huckleberry.

The group raced through the woods, with Prince Huckleberry and Queen Gingeretta following right behind Orangine. When they arrived at the cottage, they found Snow White sleeping as peacefully as she had appeared in the mirror, with the seven little friends surrounding her in sorrow.

"Oh, Snow White," whispered Queen Gingeretta, "I am so sorry for everything I've done. More than anything I wish I could undo it all." As she apologized, the queen embraced Snow White in a heartfelt hug as tears fell down her face.

And suddenly, Snow White's eyes opened! Queen Gingeretta's sincere apology and true regret had reversed her evil wishes. "What happened?" Snow White asked sleepily.

The crowd clapped and laughed with joy!

"I did something very wicked," Queen Gingeretta confessed to Snow White. "I thought that I would be the best queen—and I wanted it so badly that I put you into a deep sleep to make it happen. I'm sorry from the bottom of my heart."

Snow White hugged the queen. "I forgive you!" she exclaimed.

Later that day, there was much rejoicing in Berry Kingdom as Snow White was crowned queen.

"I am so grateful to all my friends," the new queen announced. "To Orangine for helping me; to Prince Huckleberry for finding me; and to the seven little friends who have cared for me these many days. And to Queen Gingeretta, who overcame her bad feelings to save me. I hope that you will all help me rule Berry Kingdom, as I know that you are all worthy of the task."

And so it was that Queen Snow White took the throne, joined by all her friends . . .

"...just as she was always meant to do," Strawberry Shortcake finished her story.

Her friends were quiet for a moment.

"I think I understand what that story means, Strawberry," Ginger said slowly. "Sometimes when we put ourselves first, we can end up hurting somebody else. I'm sorry. I didn't mean to say that *only* Chocolate Chipmunk was the best. I think you're all the berry best pets ever!"

"That's berry nice of you, Ginger!" exclaimed Strawberry. "And I agree. I've never known such berry wonderful pets in all my life!"

"Let's take a picture of them!" suggested Orange Blossom. The girls gathered all their pets into a group and took a picture, so that they would always remember how special their little friends were.

And they lived berry happily ever after!